This book belongs to

_____

_____

For Mortimer

tiger tales
An imprint of ME Media LLC
202 Old Ridgefield Road • Wilton, CT 06897
This paperback edition published 2003
First published in the United States 2001
Originally published in Great Britain 2001 by Little Tiger Press, London
Copyright © 2001 Ruth Galloway
ISBN-10: 1-58925-377-9
ISBN-13: 978-1-58925-377-3

Galloway, Ruth, 1973-
   Fidgety fish / by Ruth Galloway.— 1st U.S. ed.
      p. cm.
Summary: Sent out for a swim in the deep sea, Tiddler, a young fish who
just can't keep still, sees many interesting creatures and one very dark cave.
   ISBN 1-58925-012-5 (hardcover)
   ISBN 1-58925-377-9 (paperback)
[1. Fishes—Fiction. 2. Marine animals—Fiction.] I. Title.
   PZ7.G13853 Fi 2001
   [E]—dc21
                                          2001000934
Printed in the United States of America
   5 7 9 10 8 6 4

Fidgety Fish

by Ruth Galloway

tiger tales

Tiddler was always fidgeting.

He wriggled and squiggled,

he darted and giggled . . .

until his mom got fed up with him.
"Go out into the sea and swim
till you're tired, but watch out for
the Big Fish," she said.
So Tiddler swam out of his cave.

He dived and he flipped,

he leaped and he dipped.

He sped faster than a rocket...

and glided gently like a swan,
letting the sea currents fan his fins.
But he still didn't feel tired!

The sea was full of the most
interesting things.
There were limpets that clung,

and jellyfish that stung.
There was a big, big starfish
that didn't do much at all.

"Hello," said Tiddler, nudging the starfish gently with his nose. The starfish didn't answer. It didn't even move.

A crab sidled by, clicking and clacking its big claws. Tiddler wanted to play with it. But the crab scuttled off, and disappeared into the seaweed.

Tiddler came to a big, dark cave.
It looked much more exciting
than his cave back home,
and Tiddler swam in . . .

SNAP!

Everything went dark.

Tiddler was trapped inside the Big Fish!

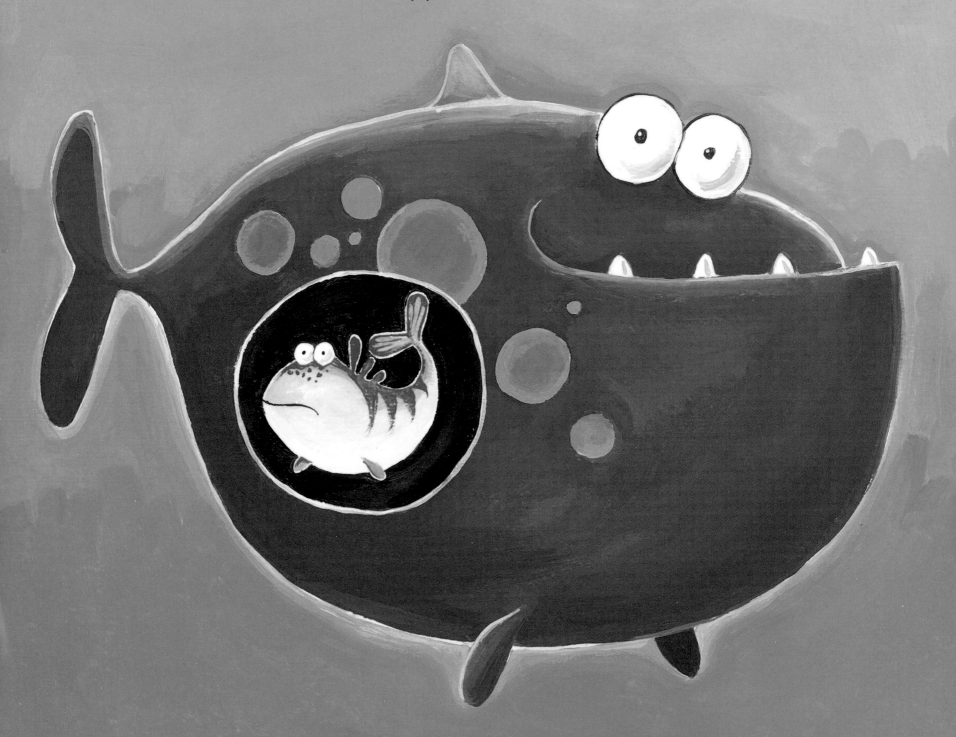

until the Big Fish's tummy began to feel very
funny indeed.

It rumbled and grumbled.
It turned and it tumbled.
It fluttered and groaned,
and mumbled and moaned.

Suddenly, the Big Fish
burped and . . .

BURP!

Out shot Tiddler.

He shot past the jellyfish and
the clickety crab hiding in the weeds...

past the starfish and straight
through his own front door!

"I hope you've used up all that energy," said his mom.

But she would have to wait until the morning to hear about his adventures, because Tiddler was already fast asleep!